TIMMY
THE LONELY
CHRISTMAS TREE

MR GREEN'S
TREE
SHOP

Written by
LIAM WHITE

Illustrated by
AMY LEONARD

This book
belongs to...

_____

In the middle of a forest,
on a hill at the **top,**

there lived a man called **Mr Green** with a Christmas tree **shop...**

He had **little** trees and **BUSHY** trees,

and trees big and **LONG,**

he had **WONKY** trees and **SPIKY** trees, and trees big and **STRONG.**

The youngest tree was called... **Billy,**

he was always scared and being **silly!**

And then there was **Timmy,**

he didn't **moan,**

all Timmy wanted was a loving **home...**

Timmy also had a friend, a sweet robin called Rosie.
"The people are here!" she said as she loved being nosey!

Soon the forest was full of people having fun,
and soon Timmy's friends were selling one by one...

One lady took a tree
to put by her
bed,

one man took a tree
to decorate his
shed.

One boy took the spiky tree for his spiky looking **mouse,**

and one man took the wonky tree for his wonky little **house.**

One little boy told
Mr Green which tree
he would **like**,

but Timmy was
just too big,
to take home on his
bike...

And one man said
Timmy was
the best tree by
far,

but Timmy was
just too big
to take home in his
car...

"Oh Rosie...

I could have lived by someone's bed, or inside someone's **shed,**

why won't anybody come and pick me **instead?"**

But just when the shop was about to **close**,
someone appeared on Timmy's **nose**...

But Timmy looked at Billy and Billy looked sad,
again he looked at Billy and Timmy felt bad.

Would Billy be okay? Would Billy understand?
Timmy felt bad so...
TIMMY MADE A PLAN!

So before the
people arrived
looking for
a tree not too
thin,

Timmy took
**A BIG
DEEP
BREATH**
...

AND
PULLED
HIS
BRANCHES
IN!

"Look at those stars!"
Mr Green said with the
shivers,

"Time to go
home to my cosy warm
slippers!"

And with that he was gone, not a person in **sight,**

just a very lonely Timmy, on Christmas Eve **night...**

All of a sudden Timmy
was covered in frost,
and suddenly Timmy felt
a little bit lost.

How Timmy longed for
some warm cosy nights,
to have a star on his head
and to be covered in lights.

"I wish I wasn't a tree,"
Timmy said to himself.
"I could have been a snowman,
or a great Christmas elf."

"Now everyone's gone,
even Rosie's flown home"
Timmy closed his eyes,
and fell asleep on his own...

Suddenly Timmy woke up by a rustle in the **leaves...**

"EXCUSE ME TIMMY!" a big voice boomed...

"WOULD YOU COME AND BE MY TREE?"
Timmy opened his eyes, and got a BIG surprise!

He saw a big red SUIT...

and big black BOOTS!

AND NEXT TO HIS SLEIGH WITH SHINY doors...

IT WAS
ONLY
MR
SANTA
CLAUSE!

And could it be?
Yes it was
true..

Rosie was
with Santa
too!

She said she had to fly to me straight **away,**

and tell me what you did for Billy **today.**

What you did was special and **kind,**

and special trees are hard to **find!**

And I'll tell you something else that's true...
I wouldn't want any other tree but
you!"

Timmy gave Santa
a hug full of
love,

"Oh Santa and Rosie,
I can't thank you
enough!"

"It's my pleasure!" Santa chuckled "and there's no need to fuss...
this wonderful little robin is coming home with us!"

So as they all flew off together, there was one thing that was sure,
Timmy the lonely Christmas tree wasn't lonely anymore.

THE END

First published in 2018 by LMW Publishing, UK
Printed in Hampshire, UK

ISBN : 978 1 5272 3155 9

Visit www.timmythetree.com
to take on Timmy's Christmas Challenge!

Like this book?
See Liam & Amy's other book,
'Hugo The Hungry Horse'